For Linda and Matthew,
with love

First U.S. edition 2004

Library of Congress Cataloging-in-Publication Data
Fearnley, Jan.
Watch out! / Jan Fearnley
p. cm.
Summary: Wilf, a very energetic mouse who gets in a bit of trouble
when he does not listen to his mother, makes her a special surprise.
ISBN 0-7636-2318-0
[1. Mother and child—Fiction. 2. Mice—Fiction. 3. Behavior—Fiction.] I. Title.
PZ7.F2965Wat 2004
[E]—dc21   2003048505

2 4 6 8 10 9 7 5 3 1

Printed in China

This book was typeset in Granjon.
The illustrations were done in watercolor and ink.

Candlewick Press
2067 Massachusetts Avenue
Cambridge, Massachusetts 02140

visit us at www.candlewick.com

CANDLEWICK PRESS
CAMBRIDGE, MASSACHUSETTS

3193193

WATCH OUT!

Jan Fearnley

Wilf was a little brown mouse, bright
as a button, and full of fun. He loved to run
and skip, and climb and play, and jump about.
From the moment the sun filled the sky
until it dozed against the hillside, Wilf was full of busy.

One day, when Wilf was busy running,
his mom said, "Watch out, Wilf!
Mind where you're going!"

Now, Wilf was a good boy.

He wanted to listen to his mom.

He really, really did . . .

but he was so busy running
that he didn't hear her!

"Look at me, Mom!"
shouted Wilf.

"I can go fast!
I'm like a
whirlwind!"

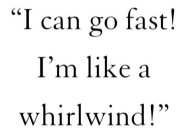

He went faster and faster and . . .

"Oh, Mommy!" said Wilf.

"Oh, Wilf," said Mom.

"I wish you'd listen to me."

Not five minutes later, Wilf was at it again. This time he was climbing up the flowers, even though they were still wet from the morning dew.

"Watch out, Wilf!" said Mom.

"Don't dangle from the dahlias!"

But Wilf didn't hear her.

He was
too busy
climbing!

"Look at me!" he cried.
"I'm a little monkey!"

"I can
climb
and climb
and climb
and . . ."

CRASH
BANG
WALLOP!

"Owww, Mommy!" said Wilf.

"Oh, Wilf," said Mom.

"I wish you'd listen to me."

Now Mom needed to do some baking.

Wilf was helping.

"Watch what you're doing with that honey," said Mom.

"We don't want it stuck on your whiskers, do we?"

But Wilf didn't hear her.
He was already
stirring the big pot
of shiny, yellow,
glossy
honey

round

and

round

and . . .

CRASH BANG
WALLOP!

Over went the table.

Over went the honey—

all over Wilf.

"Oh, Mommy!" said Wilf.

"Oh, Wilf," said Mom, as
she got the wet washcloth out.

"I wish you'd listen to me."

It was getting late, and Wilf's busy day was nearly at an end. But just before supper, Wilf decided to do some jumping in the garden.

"Watch out, Wilf!" said Mom. "Do be careful. It's very muddy."

But Wilf didn't hear her.
He was already busy—
busy jumping!

"Look at me!"
he shouted.

"I'm a wild thing!
I'm a crazy kangaroo!

I'm a
bouncy frog!

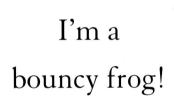

Bouncy,
bouncy,
bouncy . . ."

SPLISH SPLASH
WALLOP!

"Oh, Mommy, I'm stuck!"

"Oh, Wilf!" said Mom.
"This is a fine mess!
    There's too much crashing and
banging and not enough listening.
I wish you'd slow down, son!"

After Wilf had taken his bath,

Mom sat in her chair and had a little rest.

Wilf had a little think.

He loved his mommy very much,

and he didn't like her to be sad.

Wilf decided to make a surprise to cheer her up.

The card on the tray reads:

I Love you mommy

Very quietly (so Mom wouldn't hear),

Wilf snuck into the kitchen and made himself busy.

He made a pretty card.

He made a tray with a nice supper on it.

It was beautiful!

Wilf couldn't wait to surprise his mom.

He took his time and was ever so careful

in the kitchen . . .

down the hall . . .

right to Mom in the big chair.

"Surprise!"

he cried proudly. "I made this for you!"

Mom opened her eyes, sat up, and clapped her paws.

"Oh, my sweet boy," she cried, reaching out to Wilf.

"Come and give your mom a cuddle!"

"Watch out, Mom!" said Wilf. "Everything's wobbling!"

But Mom didn't listen!
She was too busy wanting
her cuddle and . . .

I love you
mommy

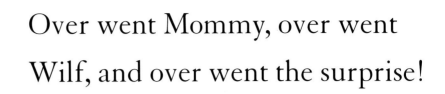

Over went Mommy, over went
Wilf, and over went the surprise!

"Oh, Mommy," said Wilf.

"Oh, Wilf," said Mom.

"Why didn't I listen to YOU?"

It was a terrible mess, but nobody minded.

"I'd still like my cuddle, if that's okay," whispered
Mom. And that's exactly what she got,
because this time, Wilf heard
every single word Mom said.